My Car by Byron Barton

Greenwillow Books, *An Imprint of HarperCollinsPublishers*

The text type is Avant Garde Gothic. Library of Congress Cataloging-in-Publication Data: Barton, Byron. My car / written and illustrated by Byron Barton.
p. cm. "Greenwillow Books." Summary: Sam describes in loving detail his car and how he drives it. ISBN 0-06-029624-0 (trade)
— ISBN 0-06-029625-9 (lib. bag.) — ISBN 0-06-058940-X (pbk.) [1. Automobiles— Fiction.] 1. Title. PZ7. B2848 My 2001 [E]—dc21 00-050334 For
information address HarperCollins Children's Books, a division of HarperCollins Publishers, 195 Broadway, New York, NY 10007.
First Edition 18 SCP 21 20 19

I
am
Sam.

This
is
my
car.

I
love
my
car.

I keep my car clean.

My
car
needs
oil

of gasoline.

My
car
has
many
parts.

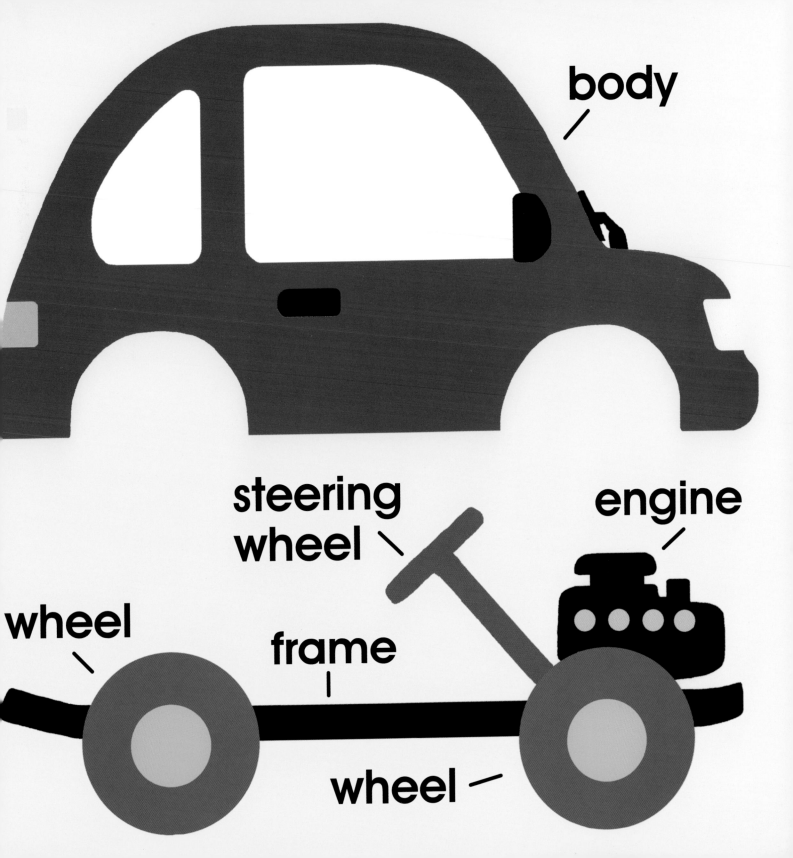

body

steering
wheel

engine

wheel

frame

wheel

My
car
has
lights
to
see
at
night

and windshield wipers

to see in the rain.

When I drive,

I drive carefully.

the laws.

WALK

I stop

for pedestrians.

MAIN ST

BUS

ONE WAY

NO PARKING

I read the signs.

I
drive
my
car
to
many
places.

I drive my car to work.

But
when
I work,

BUS

I drive